My First Experiences:

Our New Baby

Written by Catherine Mackenzie
Illustrated by Lynn Breeze
Published by Christian Focus Publications

Splat the cat is hiding in every picture in this book? Can you find him?

This is my mum and dad, my brother Tom and our cat, Splat. My name is Jane. There is a baby living inside my mum. 'Hello baby can you hear me?' I say. Mum says that the baby can hear me! 'Are babies nice?' asks Tom.

Granny has come to stay. She says a baby is a brand new, little person. Sometimes they smile. Sometimes they cry loudly. Babies need plenty of milk and lots of sleep.
We look at my baby photos. I was a baby once.

Children are a very special present from God.
Psalm 127:3

We are getting ready for the baby. The baby needs a special bed to sleep in. This is called a cot. We also have to get nappies and baby wipes and things to clean the baby with. Babies can't do much for themselves. We will all have to look after our baby.

Babies need baby jackets, and baby socks and baby hats. Babies are too small for my clothes. Babies need lots of love. We will give the baby lots of love. God will give the baby lots of love. He loves our baby even more than we do.

God is love. 1 John 4 : 16

Mum has to go to hospital all of a sudden.
The baby has decided it's time to arrive.

I wave goodbye but Granny is here so I am not on my own. Granny says mum will come back soon. I pray to God that he will keep her safe.

God will comfort you just as a mother comforts her child.   Isaiah 66:13

The next day the baby has arrived. It is a boy and we call him Matthew. I go to the hospital with Granny and the nurse takes me to see Matthew. Matthew has two blue eyes. He has ten fingers and ten toes, just like me.

The nurse tells us how much Matthew weighs and how long he is. Matthew also has a special name tag on his wrist. This is so the nurses and doctors know which baby belongs to which mum.

I am fearfully and wonderfully made.
Psalm 139:14

Mum and Dad take Matthew home. We clean him up and mum gives him some milk to drink. I feel jealous of baby Matthew. He gets presents and cuddles and songs sung to him. It's not fair.

But I should love my baby brother all the time. Jesus loves me and this makes me smile.

I will tell Matthew that Jesus loves him.

Train a child in the way they should go.
Proverbs 22:6

Matthew is put in his cot. It is time for him to sleep. But I am big and I don't have to go to bed yet. Dad takes me and Tom to the park. We swing on the swings and go 'Whhhheeeee' down the slide.

Then we all feel hungry and go home for something to eat. Sausages, chips and beans are my favourite food. Babies aren't allowed sausages for their tea!

Every good and perfect gift comes from God.
James 1:17

Before I go to sleep mum says a prayer with me. We thank God for Matthew. I get a hug and a story. Mum says she is glad I am big and responsible. I will help her and Matthew.

Tomorrow we will put Matthew in his pram. Then we will all go for a walk together. Mum will teach me a new song to sing to Matthew. It will help him go to sleep. It will be a song about how much Jesus loves us all. Thank you Jesus for my family.

God has put a new song in my mouth.
A song of praise to him. Psalm 40:3

You can sing a song about Jesus too.
This song is about how much Jesus loves us.

Jesus loves me - this I know
For the Bible tells me so.
Little ones to him belong.
We are weak but he is strong.

Yes, Jesus loves me!
Yes, Jesus loves me!
Yes, Jesus loves me!
The Bible tells me so.

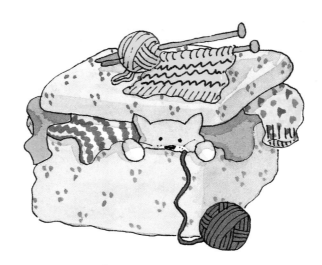